A Crabby Book

Hello, Crabby!

Jonathan Fenske

For Pendy, who still laughs
at my dad jokes.

Published in the UK by Scholastic Children's Books, 2020

Euston House, 24 Eversholt Street, London, NW1 1DB, UK

A division of Scholastic Limited.

London – New York – Toronto – Sydney – Auckland

Mexico City – New Delhi – Hong Kong

SCHOLASTIC and associated logos are trademarks and/or

registered trademarks of Scholastic Inc.

First published in the US by Scholastic Inc, 2019

Text illustration © Jonathan Fenske, 2019

The right of Jonathan Fenske to be identified as the author and illustrator of this work has
been asserted by him under the Copyright, Designs and Patents Act 1988.

ISBN 978 0 702 30082 0

A CIP catalogue record for this book is available from the British Library.

Printed by CPI Group (UK) Ltd, Croydon, CR0 4YY

Papers used by Scholastic Children's Books are made

from wood grown in sustainable forests.

1 3 5 7 9 10 8 6 4 2

www.scholastic.co.uk

2

3

Hmmm.
What exciting thing
can I do today?

I can dig
a hole.

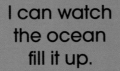

I can watch
the ocean
fill it up.

I can dig
a hole
again.

4

I can scuttle to the dunes.

I can scuttle to the water.

I can sit **right here**.

Wow.

So many choices.

Well, it looks like today is a **SCUTTLE-TO-THE-WATER** day.

THINGS TO DO:
scuttle to the water

15

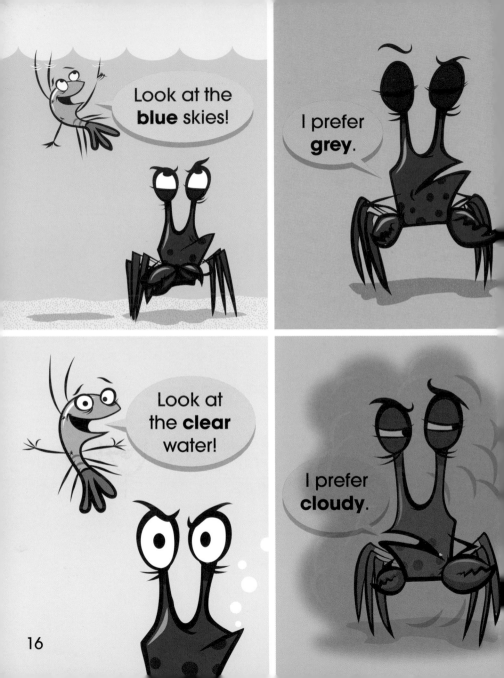

Well, Abby is a crab. And **she** is not crabby.

La, la, la!

Tabby is a crab. And **she** is not crabby.

La, la, la!

Blabby is a crab. And **he** is not crabby.

La, la, la!

Blah, blah, blah!

19

21

So, you would probably **not** be crabby if I told you a really funny joke?

No. It is probably **not** a really funny joke.

I **promise** it will tickle your funny bone!

23

That was the joke?

I told you it wasn't funny.

AAARGH!

Let me show you how this works.

25

THE CAKE

Hello, Crabby!

If I told you I baked you an **awesome** cake, would you still be crabby?

30

31

33

38

GASP!

GASP! GASP!

And for the record, I prefer **lemon** cake.

So, are you going to eat some cake?

I was not planning on it.

TAP
TAP

TWITCH
TWITCH

Oh, all right.
Give me some cake.

About the Author

Jonathan Fenske lives in South Carolina with his family. He was born in Florida near the ocean, so he knows all about life at the beach! Sea creatures never baked him a cake, but he would have **loved** Plankton's cake because chocolate is his favourite flavour.

Jonathan is the author and illustrator of several children's books including **Barnacle Is Bored**, **Plankton Is Pushy** (a Junior Library Guild selection), and the LEGO® picture book **I'm Fun, Too!** His early reader **A Pig, a Fox, and a Box** was a Theodor Seuss Geisel Honour Book.

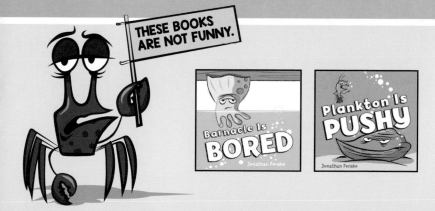

THESE BOOKS ARE NOT FUNNY.

Barnacle Is BORED
Jonathan Fenske

Plankton Is PUSHY
Jonathan Fenske

YOU CAN DRAW CRABBY!

YIPPEE.

1. Draw two ovals and connect them with a "U" to make eyes.

2. Draw the body.

3. Add six legs and one mouth.

4. Draw two arms and two claws. (One claw should be bigger.)

5. Add the details.

6. Colour in your drawing!

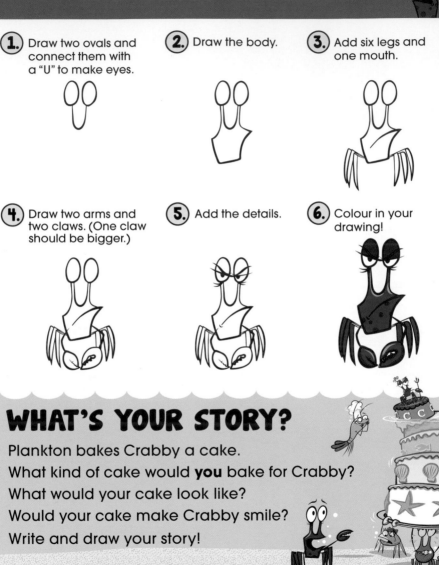

WHAT'S YOUR STORY?

Plankton bakes Crabby a cake.

What kind of cake would **you** bake for Crabby?

What would your cake look like?

Would your cake make Crabby smile?

Write and draw your story!